Y0-BGD-290

WITHDRAWN

LEARNING RESOURCES CENTER
UNIVERSITY OF WYOMING LIBRARIES
LARAMIE, WY 82071

394.2
Nal

Celebrations
of
African Heritage

WARREN J. HALLIBURTON

EDITED BY
SUSAN M. GROSSMAN

CRESTWOOD HOUSE
NEW YORK

MAXWELL MACMILLAN CANADA
TORONTO

MAXWELL MACMILLAN INTERNATIONAL
NEW YORK OXFORD SINGAPORE SYDNEY

AFRICA TODAY AFRICA TODAY AFRICA TODAY AFRICA TODAY AFRICA TODAY AFRICA TODAY AFRICA TODAY

ACKNOWLEDGMENTS

All photos courtesy of Magnum Photos.

Special thanks to Laura Straus for her assistance in putting this project together.

PHOTO CREDITS: COVER: *Ian Berry; Dennis Stock* 4, 8, 19, 33, 34;
Ian Berry 6, 9, 18, 20, 23, 30, 32, 35, 37, 38; *Steve McCurry* 7;
George Rodger 10; *Bruno Barbey* 12, 15, 16, 26, 28;
Marilyn Silverstone 25; *Rene Burri* 40;
Eve Arnold 43; *Stuart Franklin* 44

Cover design, text design and production: William E. Frost Associates Ltd.

Library of Congress Cataloging-in-Publication Data

Halliburton, Warren J.
    Celebrations of African heritage / by Warren Halliburton;
edited by Susan M. Grossman. — 1st ed.
    p. cm. — (Africa today)
    Summary: Examines the different ways in which African heritage is
    celebrated, both in the United States and in Africa, in such areas as
    religious practices, art, music, dance, and storytelling.
    ISBN 0-89686-676-9
    1. Afro-Americans — Social life and customs — Juvenile literature. 2.
    Africa — Social life and customs — Juvenile literature. 3. Rites and
    ceremonies — United States — Juvenile literature. 4. Rites and
    ceremonies — Africa — Juvenile literature [1. Afro-Americans —
    Social life and customs. 2. Africa — Social life and customs.] I.
    Grossman, Susan M. II. Title. III. Series: Africa today
E185.86.H25 1992
394.2 — dc20   92-7989

Copyright © 1992 by CRESTWOOD HOUSE, MACMILLAN PUBLISHING COMPANY

All rights reserved. No part of this book may be reproduced or transmitted in any form or by any
means, electronic or mechanical, including photocopying, recording, or by any information
storage and retrieval system, without permission in writing from the Publisher.

CRESTWOOD HOUSE   MAXWELL MACMILLAN CANADA, INC.
MACMILLAN PUBLISHING COMPANY   1200 Eglinton Avenue East
866 Third Avenue   Suite 200
New York, NY 10022   Don Mills, Ontario M3C 3N1

Macmillan Publishing Company is part of the Maxwell Communication Group of Companies.
First edition
Printed in the United States of America

1   2   3   4   5   6   7   8   9   10

Contents

NOTE: The images in this book are meant to convey visually the spirit of the African arts, and are therefore not captioned. For full descriptions of the photos *see page 46*.

Introduction

A Cherished Heritage

On the night after Christmas, an African-American family and the friends they have invited to their home gather around a table decorated in black, red and green. These colors symbolize Africa: black for the beauty of the people, red for the blood of the ancestors and green for the fertility of the land. On a *mkeke*, a hand-woven mat, sits a basket filled with *mazao*, tropical fruits and vegetables that represent thanksgiving for the harvest. Surrounding the basket are *vibunzi* — ears of corn — one to celebrate each child in the family, because Africans say that children are a person's wealth. One of the children lights the central black candle of the *kinara*, the candelabra whose seven candles represent the seven principles of *Nguzo Saba*, the values that reunite African-Americans with their heritage. The family recites the first principle — unity — before passing around the *Kikombe*, the cup that represents community unity and

5

LEARNING RESOURCES CENTER
UNIVERSITY OF WYOMING LIBRARIES
LARAMIE, WY 82071

honors the ancestors. Then they sit down to the table, which is barely visible under platters of American and African food, and break their daylong fast.

This family is celebrating **Kwanzaa**, a holiday created in 1966 to pay tribute to the cultural roots of Americans of African ancestry. The name comes from the phrase *mantundda ya kwanza*, which means "first fruits of the harvest" in Swahili, a language spoken throughout East Africa. The holiday, which occurs on the seven days following Christmas and ends on New Year's Day, is based on traditional African harvest festivals. On each of the seven nights, the family will gather with their friends and relatives to feast, exchange gifts, and learn about African culture and their personal history. On each night, a new candle will be lit, and the family will talk about the idea it represents. The principles Kwanzaa celebrates are those that are traditionally valued in Africa: community unity; self-determination — doing the right thing; collective work and responsibility; cooperative economics, helping one another and the community; and purpose, meaning each person's purpose

7

and importance, to him- or herself and to one another. On the sixth night, gifts are exchanged. On the final night, the last candle is lit for *imani* — faith, in oneself and one's ancestors.

The heritage shared by people of African descent all over the world is rich and deep. Africa is a land where history and faith have for thousands of years been expressed in art, music, story and song. It is also a hard land where nature can bring benefit or disaster. It has been subjected to a history of **colonization**, sometimes brutal, by other powers, and must deal with its own turbulent political and economic troubles. It is a continent that has been forced to undergo in the last generation change that in other places evolved over hundreds of years. It is a place struggling to find a balance between its vibrant past and a future whose course is not yet clear.

In the face of all this change, Africans continue to celebrate their joys and use their tradition and faith to uphold themselves in troubled times. And while traditional practices are being changed by the times, they also absorb elements of modern life and translate the new world into understandable designs, creating a lively patchwork of tradition and modern life that has the potential to be as beautiful as the patterns of old.

Religions of Africa

In the Beginning

The Akamba say that God asked the chameleon, who is intelligent and truthful, to tell humans that they would rise again after they had died. But the weaverbird, who is a liar, reached humans first and told them that all people would perish forever, and the magpie, who listened to both, told humans that the weaverbird was right. Thus Death came into the world.

But the Khoi say that it was the moon who sent the messenger to humans, and that the messenger was an insect, and it was the hare that fooled the insect and told humans that they would die — as the moon did when day came — and the moon split the hare's nose in punishment.

And the Ashantis say that the lesser gods are descended from a small child who outwitted both the Sky God and Death, and when a human whom Death wishes to take appeals to the lesser gods, Death may spare that person.

Traditional Religions

In general, the world's religions probably developed as efforts to control and explain nature, and the religions of Africa share these origins. Africa is a hard place for people to live in. It ranges between flood and drought, desert and rain forest. Where the land is dry, it is difficult to grow food; where it is wet, waterborne diseases rage. It is no wonder that, in this beautiful but harsh place where fortune depends so much upon the whims of nature, religion developed to address the spirits of nature to ask for their help or to avert disaster. Thus followers of traditional African religions might sacrifice an ox to the powers, as the Dinka people do, to encourage them to heal a sick person, or pray to Shango, a West African spirit of fire and lightning, to ask that a storm not damage their village.

About 40 percent of Africans are Muslims, and almost half of the Muslims in Africa live in northern Africa — Egypt, Libya, Tunisia, Algeria, Morocco and Sudan. About 13 percent of Africans are Christian, a tiny percentage is Jewish, Hindu, or Sikh, and the rest follow traditional religions. There is a multitude of different peoples — Nigeria alone has 250 ethnic groups — in Africa and as many belief systems. Even the followers of Christianity and Islam practice those religions in ways unique to their different backgrounds. Most traditional African religions, however, have certain elements in common.

Unlike the **monotheistic** religions of Christianity, Judaism, and Islam, traditional African religions are **pantheistic** — that is, they acknowledge the divinity of more than one being. Most traditional religions recognize one supreme god or creator, with a hierarchy of lesser gods and spirits. For instance, the Yoruba, the largest ethnic group in West Africa with a population of 12 million, worship a high god, Olorun. Under Olorun are Orishas, spirit messengers — Shango is a major Orisha. There is an Orisha for every occasion, and to each is dedicated a shrine and priest who directs the festivals that regularly honor the spirit, as well as sacrifices and prayer for specific purposes. Gods can be brought into being by other gods, or they can even be humans who, when they were alive, were considered to have special powers — Shango, for instance, is said to have been a chief whose people seemed never to be harmed by storms. Ancestors are the lowest level of divinity, and they may be asked in prayer to deliver requests to higher levels of powers.

This is a simplification, however, of complex ideas. It is more accurate to say that most religions recognize a divine force that inhabits everything in the universe, and what are called gods are manifestations of this divine force. The Nilotic peoples of East Africa call this **Jok**. Jok dwells in the wind; the soul is Jok; and God is the greatest Jok of all.

Thus traditional African religion is **animistic**: It contains the idea that everything in the universe — water, plants, animals, rocks, the

13

LEARNING RESOURCES CENTER
UNIVERSITY OF WYOMING LIBRARIES
LARAMIE, WY 82071

earth itself — has a soul. In this belief system, spirit is a part of all objects, so objects can be endowed with specific powers or properties. These objects, called **fetishes**, are a large part of African religion.

Any object can be a fetish and possess magical powers. These powers can be inserted into an object by the act of performing the proper magical rites over it. Statues are fetishes but any other object can be one as well: a feather, a stone, a string of beads. Every fetish has a particular function, so many Africans wear several fetishes in a bag around their necks.

Ancestor statues are special fetishes reserved for rituals involving ancestors. They can be used to appease an angry spirit, cure sickness believed to be caused by a hostile ancestor, ask for the ancestor's help in a task, or bestow forgiveness.

A fetish that has meaning for an entire group is a **totem**. Totems are usually animals. Africans who are members of communities that claim brotherhood with the spirits contained in certain animals will not kill those animals.

In these ways, religion was — and is — a powerful force woven into everyday African life, so much so that when the religions of Africa met Islam and Christianity, traditional beliefs and customs were often blended with the new philosophies and practices.

This is especially true of Islam in West Africa, where many great leaders and religious figures have been Africans. However, the result of absorbing Islam into many different belief systems is that Islam is practiced in many different ways, and this has led to violent confrontations between groups that do not have the same beliefs and customs.

Islam and Christianity

Islam was brought into Egypt in the seventh century and in less than 100 years had spread from the Middle East across northern Africa into Spain. Although **conversion** in North Africa was by conquest, the religion moved across the continent largely through the influence of traveling merchants and scholars.

Before the development of Islam, a form of Christianity known as Coptic Christianity was observed in Egypt and Ethiopia. This belief system includes elements of ancient Judaism, such as **circumcision** and

ritual cleanliness. Coptic Christianity remains the major religion in Ethiopia and has millions of followers throughout the rest of Africa as well.

Today, Islam is strongest in North Africa and in parts of West and East Africa. It is a minority religion in the middle of the continent, and it is hardly a force at all in southern Africa.

Islam brought subtle changes in concepts as well as large changes in the ways in which Africans worshiped. Africans who thought of their village as the world were forced to realize that the world included distant places, since as Muslims they were required to undertake a **pilgrimage** to Mecca. Islam brought an awareness of clocks and calendars to societies that did not emphasize an awareness of time. Islam brought a structured legal system and a focus on the written word, and schools in which to learn formally about these concepts. It imposed a common language, Arabic, on the countries of northern Africa.

While Islam had a strong impact on the religious life of Africa, the Christian missionary movement's greater effect was on economic and social structures. Christianity has to some extent been absorbed by traditional religions without completely replacing them. For instance, many peoples simply accepted the cross as a fetish. And when a woman of the healing Zaar Cult in Khartoum dances, the spirit who is believed to speak and move through her is as likely to be the Virgin Mary as that of a leopard.

Although the missionary movement, which was most active in the 18th and 19th centuries, established hospitals and refugee camps, the missionary schools designed to teach Christian values had the drawback of degrading traditional African values and customs. Partly in reaction to that degradation, a movement arose to "Africanize" the ideas of Christianity. Independent churches, such as the Kimbanguist Church in central Africa with four million followers, were formed. This church, based in Zaire, portrays Jesus as an African. Since women play important roles in many traditional belief systems of that area, women may hold important church positions. Other churches emphasize music and dance in worship and communal prayer for the purpose of faith healing.

There is a Jewish population in southern Africa, but many of the Jews of northern Africa, who emigrated from Spain and Portugal in the 15th and 16th centuries, have relocated as a result of the Arab-Israeli conflicts. Most of Ethiopia's Falasha Jews were airlifted to Israel in the mid-1980s to escape famine; about 8,000 remain. Even in Israel, the Falashas maintain traditional African practices.

The religious life of Africa, with its many influences, is a colorful stew of different beliefs and customs, and it pervades the day-to-day activities of most people. As in all other facets of African life, the challenge is in preserving tradition while acknowledging change.

2

Celebrations of Ethnic Heritage

The Living Past

Four hundred warriors of the Masai, a people who are still largely **nomadic** herdsmen of the East African plain, gather for the Eunoto ceremony, which marks their passage into elderhood. These young men were all circumcised together some 14 years ago. Since then, they have roamed the Serengeti Plain, hunting, raiding for cattle and finding girlfriends. Now they are ready to marry, start a family and build the cattle herd that is the mark of status and wealth among their people. They paint their bodies with chalk in designs that reflect their powers as warriors. The youths who have killed lions wear a lions'-mane headdress, and those who have not wear a headdress of ostrich feathers. At the conclusion of the ceremony, the young men's heads are shaved, and they trade their bright clothing for a blanket — never again to wear the headdress and finery of the warrior.

This is but one of the countless ceremonies carried out by the many peoples of Africa. Ethnic affiliations and traditions are a powerful force among the almost 600 million people of this continent who come from 1,000 different ethnic groups, each with its own sets of beliefs and customs and many with their own language. In northern Africa, ethnic groups are organized into smaller units called tribes.

There are still many groups that maintain traditional ways of life that have not been greatly altered by the changes that have taken place in the past century. Eighty-five percent of Africans still live in villages associated with their people, and even as nomads take up settled lives and villagers move into cities, people tend to identify themselves with clan, tribe, or people rather than with the state. They continue to hold on to many of their customs.

In many groups, rites of passage — birth, death, the attainment of adulthood, marriage — are marked by elaborate rites and celebrations. The passage into adulthood, for instance, varies among different groups but has some common features. In general, this time requires a period of preparation. The initiates may wear special clothing or paint their faces or bodies. The ritual might include isolation — in some groups, the young people awaiting initiation can be seen in public only if they are wearing something that covers them from head to foot. There is usually a period of instruction by elders, often in song and dance, in what is proper behavior for each sex.

The endurance of pain is a widespread feature of initiation. Often this takes the form of circumcision, which a boy or young man is expected to bear without anesthetic and without showing pain. (An increasing number of young African men compromise with tradition and have their circumcisions done in hospitals.) In a small number of groups, including some Muslim societies, women are "circumcised" as well. This involves removing some of the structures of the vagina, and may involve sewing up the opening of the vagina. It is a very painful procedure and can result in discomfort for a woman's entire lifetime. Only after circumcision are the youths considered true men and women and eligible for marriage. In many East African tribes, a boy or girl might be **scarified** — have patterns carved into their faces or

bodies. For instance, boys of the Dinka, whose life revolves around their cattle, have the shape of horns cut into their foreheads.

Clothing and jewelry often carries messages in African tribal society. Zulu girls of southern Africa weave messages, conveyed by color, into beaded bands they give their boyfriends. The color of beads or number of strands an East African woman wears might indicate her

LEARNING RESOURCES CENTER
UNIVERSITY OF WYOMING LIBRARIES
LARAMIE, WY 82071

age, marital status, whether she can bear children, or even more specific information. Detail on a piece of clothing or jewelry can advertise social status or wealth. The placement of jewelry can carry messages — brass amulets worn on the lower arm of a Rendille man means that he is married, but amulets worn on the upper arm say that his first son has been circumcised.

Hail to the Chief

In some areas, particularly along the West African coast — Ghana, Benin, Nigeria, Cameroon, the Congo — there were kingships with an elaborate court life, and much ceremony still revolves around the chiefs of different regions. Although in most African states the formal power of government is now vested in a head of state, usually a president (Morocco, Swaziland, and Lesotho are still monarchies), the chiefs still hold great political, social and religious power over the regions for which they are responsible, and in some states the chiefs have been absorbed into the present-day government. The chief is the living representative of the ancestors, extending protection to the people, and is so honored. The Oba of Benin, for instance, wears coral beads because coral is supposed to protect the fertility of the land, and this trait is renewed by washing the coral in blood every year.

The ceremonies are reminders, as well, of the chief's authority. At ceremonial gatherings, minstrels, horn blowers, drummers, and court criers proclaim the success of the chief's ancestors and remind everyone that the chief is their descendant. The chief's inherited regalia is a further reminder of this fact. Funerals are important occasions, with dancers and feasts. When an Ashanti chief dies, the highly trained young women who dance at his funeral wear gold jewelry so elaborate that it may take them two days to dress. Everyone else in the village wears red or black robes.

In other types of societies, longevity is considered more important than position or wealth. The headman is often the oldest man in the village. His job is to make sacrifices to protect the people and to influence God and the spirits to provide good health, rain, successful hunting and a good harvest.

Celebrations of Nature

The rhythm of rural life revolves around the seasons. Tasks that are appropriate for one season may be disastrous in another — a Dowayo potter, in northern Cameroon, would never make a pot in the rainy season for fear of endangering the whole village. All over Africa, festivals are celebrated to mark natural events. In Burkina Faso (formerly Upper Volta), dancers wear masks to celebrate the harvest. The Muslim Berber tribes of the Maghreb, the region of mountains, valleys and desert between the sea and the Sahara, celebrate the three-day Imilchil fair when the harvest is safely in. It provides an opportunity to sell livestock, and more important for these people who travel in small family groups, it is a chance for men and women to meet and marry. The Tuaregs of the Sahel, which borders the Sahara, bring their animals to eat salty new grass after the August and September rains bring salt to the surface of the soil, and they celebrate this meeting time with dancing, singing, feasting and camel races.

Celebrations of bonds and belonging go on all over Africa in different ways, from celebrations in a family shrine all the way up to the level of affairs of state. Change proceeds at a headlong rate in Africa, but tradition endures and accommodates as well.

Art

The manager of a shop specializing in West African art points to a tall wooden statue. "People ask these objects for help. A long time ago, this man was able to speak to the spirit world. But when he died, he took all his secrets with him. Nobody knew how to get in touch with the underworld, and things were very bad. So they made a statue of him, and instead of performing the rites themselves, they prayed to the statue and asked it to intercede on their behalf. And things were good again."

He picks up a small wooden statue that looks like a mermaid. "This is Mammy Water," he says. "When the flood waters rise, people pray to her to make them pull back. And they do."

The manager looks at a pair of statues of children. "These are fertility statues. When a mother is barren, she obtains one of these and

cuddles it and carries it with her in a sling as she would her own child. If she does this, she will conceive.

"I know it's hard to believe, but these things work. They make things happen."

The Message of Art

The art of Africa is intimately tied to the religion of Africa. Because African religion (other than Islam) was not transmitted in written form, religious ideas had to be conveyed in other ways. The traditional purpose of art was to convey a message about people's relation to nature and the spirit world. For instance, a sculpture could represent an ancestor, who could then be asked to relay a request to the underworld or embody a spirit who could placate nature or make something good happen, as in the previous examples.

Traditional artists usually work within a framework of features that an object representing a particular spirit, force, idea or ancestor must have. Within that framework, however, they have creative freedom, so works of art are never identical. And people do sometimes decorate items purely for the sake of beauty.

In general, people in areas where natural conditions allowed them to settle produced monumental items like sculptures and masks. The seminomadic people of East Africa could not carry large items with them, so much of their artistic expression is in clothing, jewelry, hairstyles, and other types of body ornamentation. The San, or Bushmen, of southern Africa left rock paintings in the desert, and rock paintings can also be found in the deserts and steppes of northern and eastern Africa. Some of these paintings — depicting herds, hunting scenes, rituals, the mythology of the San — are 10,000 years old. In North Africa, where Islam is the dominant religion, representational art — art that shows an object — is forbidden, so art takes the form of elaborate design.

Sculpture

Sculptures are the medium between people and the spirit world. Ancestor sculptures embody the spirit of the tribe and are very specific to the tribe that creates them. They must have the features that are

most beautiful to that group so that the spirit will be pleased and make a dwelling in the sculpture. The spirit must be honored periodically with prayer and sacrifice or it will leave. Large statues, worshiped on special occasions, usually belong to the community and are cared for by a priest. Smaller figures may be personal property, kept in a household shrine.

Masks

Masks allow the spirits of the dead or the protective spirits of a community to have a place to appear during dramatic performances of myths. They are often frightening, combining animal and human features. Small masks may be used as sacred objects, or they may be worn like pins or charms as badges of secret societies. The masks, like the sculptures, are consecrated — made holy — by the performance of rituals, and the wearer borrows the power of the spirit when he or she dances. They are worn at funerals, where they honor the dead and cleanse the village of any evil forces associated with the death. Masks are also often worn by village officials — for instance, when they must make a judgment.

LEARNING RESOURCES CENTER
UNIVERSITY OF WYOMING LIBRARIES
LARAMIE, WY 82071

Elements of Decoration

Even everyday objects often have some connection with the spirit world. Animals, ancestors or spirits may be carved into musical instruments, spoons, knives, bowls and tools, for example. Sometimes the object is carved with a geometric pattern that may stand for something. Symbols are different for different groups. For example, the zigzag pendant worn by women in northern Africa represents a hand to ward off the evil eye. But in West Africa, zigzag designs stand for, among other things, lightning, water, or a snake, which in turn have connotations — or sometimes it's just a decoration. Human features, such as a face,

carved into the handle of a spoon are common — and often refer to a myth.

Animals — commonly antelopes, chameleons, snakes, elephants, spiders, birds, leopards and monkeys — are also often connected with mythology, although a particular animal won't mean the same thing for every group. The animal may also be used to represent a certain quality: strength for an elephant, long life for a tortoise. Sometimes only one feature of the animal is used. For instance, the Berbers, who as Muslims cannot depict an animal, often include in their art a snake's head, for fertility, or a jackal's paw, for healing, among symbols of other animals.

The Art of Royalty

Where there were powerful kingships — such as in Nigeria, Cameroon, Zaire, and Ghana — the purpose of art, in the form of furniture, jewelry, instruments, and clothing, was often to say something about status. In northern Ghana, the skins a king sat on were symbols of kingship — the fiercer the animal, the greater the chief. In the south, the stool was the symbol of royal status, and the presidential throne of the Republic of Ghana is still in the shape of the traditional stool. Other stools and chairs were carved for ceremonial purposes.

In the absence of written history, the inherited items a king owned and the things he wore conveyed his history. Important officials still wear traditional regalia on state occasions such as robes of *kente* cloth, (which is handwoven in small strips by men and sewn together by women and is too costly for average people to own) hats, necklaces, rings and sandals with gold decorations. The meaning of these items is so specific that an official can indicate that he's changed his mind simply by changing his clothing.

In these places, too, secret societies arose, and many pieces of art were produced as cult objects used in worship. The work of the Yoruba includes many of these objects: ceremonial staffs with cowrie shells for fertility, bowls and platters for divination, ceremonial axes shaped like animals, carved boxes for holding substances used in ceremonies, spirit masks, and figures of gods in precious substances like gold and ivory.

Material

Wood is often used for making statues and masks. Masks may be painted, most often in black-and-white — white is the color of the spirits. Some groups decorate their statues and masks with jewelry, beads, shells (especially cowrie), leather or horns. Other artists work in metal. The artists of West Africa are known for casting objects in gold, copper, bronze and brass. Other groups in East and West Africa work in iron.

The Art Scene Today

Africa has a rich artistic history. But Africa has undergone much change in the last century, and it is the nature of art to reflect the society that produces it. Although there are still artists working in time-honored forms, others are using their heritage to produce new kinds of work and express the changes and conflicts occurring in their world.

Some artists handle traditional subject matter in new ways and use nontraditional materials. For instance, there are artists who work in concrete to produce statues reminiscent of West African sculpture. Other artists use traditional materials to create new forms — in addition to beading their clothing, the Zulu women of Thousand Hills Valley in South Africa use beads and cloth to make sculptures that express truths about their way of life and the turbulent politics of their land.

The changing times have also brought changes in how Africans think about art and its purpose. Art for profit, divorced from community need, is a relatively new concept, and increasingly few craftsmen have the training, time, and source of income to produce traditional art. Many are saddened by this fact, but it will be exciting to see how today's artists, combining heritage with modern life, will create their own traditions.

Celebrations in Story, Dance and Song

The Oral Tradition

On a moonlit night in a Benga village in West Africa, people gather around the fire to hear their best storyteller relate the story of why Bat lives alone. He describes how Bat asked Antelope for medicine to cure his sick mother and how Antelope told him to ask Joba, the Sun. The audience shouts the refusal Joba made for six days. The storyteller describes the mourning feast Bat prepares for all the animals when his mother dies on the seventh day. The old man uses his hands and body to become all sorts of animals as he tells how Bat asked the beasts to help him bury his mother and gives the beasts' answer: "This person has wings and is obviously a bird." He becomes a bird when he gives the birds' answer: "This person has teeth and therefore is not one of us." The audience groans when he gives Bat's conclusion: "I am not a beast and not a bird. I will live by myself and never look on them in the daylight, for none will claim me and Sun didn't help me." The storyteller asks his audience, "Is Bat a beast or a bird?" A lively debate follows.

The education of young people in Africa traditionally took place in this informal way. Children hearing this story would learn many things. They would get an explanation of a particular animal's habits, learn that it is important to care for and honor parents, and understand that the community is responsible to its members.

Children listening to their elders tell fables learned about ethics, morality and acceptable behavior. Statements are made in proverbs: "Even if you sit on the bottom of the sea, you cannot be a fish," a mother in Sierra Leone might warn an overambitious child. People listening to myths learned about nature, festivals, rituals, and the organization and elements of their religion. Sacred stories transmitted information necessary in rites of passage. Tales about heroes emphasized the unity and value of the group.

The growing emphasis on writing and formal education has changed the place of oral tradition in society. But new ways are being found to integrate tradition with technology — stories once told in the village square are now told over the radio. That method lacks the lively feedback and intergenerational give-and-take of the storyteller, but it provides one compromise between the past and the future as African parents and teachers look for ways to continue to transmit traditional values.

Dance

Six very young women dressed in long blue and brown tunics are performing a *laamba*, a healing dance from Senegal. Their white skirts fly up around their knees as they jump into the air. Their beads rattle in time with their rhythm. As one woman steps forward, her pace becomes even faster. Arms reaching upward, bare feet stamping, she barely seems to be earthbound. As she jumps a final time, her beads fly over her head and sail through the air, as exuberant and colorful as the young dancer.

Dance is yet another way of transmitting history and tradition. The dancer is an artist who tells a story with his or her movements and

costume. The dancer can become an animal, a spirit, a character, or an ancestor. Masked dancers act out myths at festivals and religious celebrations. The fantastic masks and headdresses endow the dancers with the spirits they are believed to house, so that dancers can truly seem to be possessed, immune to exhaustion and pain.

Dances are performed on occasions of state affairs — on ceremonial days in Zaire, the wives of a Mangbetu chief dance in skirts of black-and-white monkey fur. Dance is a part of funeral observance: When the supreme chief of the Bamilikes in Cameroon dies, members of the secret elephant-mask society perform, wearing beaded elephant masks that cover their faces. There are dances for the harvest and for the hunt. Dance is the language of love: Moorish women dance the Guedra, a ritual ballet that involves moving only the hands and feet. People celebrate all kinds of gatherings and occasions with dance.

Dance and theater have been used to express feelings about political situations over which people otherwise have little control. During the period of colonialism, masked dancers underscored traditional values and made fun of Europeans.

The rhythms of African dance have traveled around the world: the rhumba, the Brazilian samba, America's tap and jazz. In turn, the rhythms of the world have influenced dance in urban Africa. And traditional dance lives on in rural Africa.

Music

Traditionally, African music, like other arts of Africa, had among its purposes to express life truthfully and to convey information. This could be very literal: The kings of the Yoruba, who have a melodic language close to singing, included in their court drummers whose drums imitated the tones of speech. That way the drummers could announce who was at the gates long before a person reached the palace. Very few kings can afford to maintain court drummers anymore since they can no longer collect taxes, but music in Africa still often has a purpose other than to make a pleasant sound. Politicians use music as part of their campaigns. The people express political viewpoints in song. The traditional *oriki*, songs of praise traditionally written for rulers and also for gods, cities, plants and animals, are now as likely to be songs about the rich and famous played by *juju* bands.

Music is an area in which tradition has very directly influenced contemporary forms. By the same token, contemporary life has influenced and changed traditional forms. Modern bands include ancient instruments at the same time that tribal musicians are introducing electronic instruments into their repertoires. Backup dancers might perform in modern dress or traditional dress. Bembeya Jazz, a group from Guinea, base their work on the melodies and rhythms of Mandingo music. Some *griots*, the traditional minstrels of the Sudan who sang at various important social and court functions, now sing on the radio. Other griots still follow the tradition of performing at feasts, weddings and funerals, but many are finding it difficult to make a living as the lifestyle that supported their role in society changes.

In America, African music influenced the development of jazz in the early 20th century. Contemporary musicians such as Paul Simon and Peter Gabriel have backed their work up with African folk rhythms and instruments. African musicians performing in the United States are finding an enthusiastic audience. Afro-pop, with its Nigerian roots, lively rhythms and often political lyrics, can be heard on American radio. People pack clubs to sway to the hypnotic beat of reggae. The links between past and present remain strong, and the world has benefited from learning the rhythms of Africa.

LEARNING RESOURCES CENTER
UNIVERSITY OF WYOMING LIBRARIES
LARAMIE, WY 82071

The Future

Many people — both in Africa and in other places — mourn the loss of traditional ways. But Africa is not a museum. It is a vital continent with a rich heritage and a future that must be faced. It is to be hoped that today's emerging Africa will bring with it the best of its past to discover a new and equally vibrant way of life.

PHOTO IDENTIFICATION

(COVER) dancers\Ghana; (**4**) a parade\Ghana; (**6**) dancers\Ghana; (**7**) members of the Wodaabe herdsmen\Niger; (**8**) a traditional wedding\Ghana; (**9**) a funeral\Liberia; (**10**) a voodoo ceremony\Ghana; (**12**) tribal dancers\Nigeria; (**15**) a bronzeworker\Nigeria; (**16**) a mourning ceremony\Nigeria; (**18**) a festival for the dead\Mali; (**19**) a parade\Ghana; (**20**) Ashanti tribesmen greet their new king\Ghana; (**23**) a mask carver\Mali; (**25**) an Aburi festival\Ghana; (**26**) a nomadic fair\Morocco; (**28**) making a bronze statue\Cameroon; (**30**) a sculptor\Cameroon; (**32**) a sculptor\Cameroon; (**33**) a spirit mask\Ghana; (**34**) a kente cloth shop\Ghana; (**35**) detail of a carving\Cameroon; (**37**) a brass scepter\Ghana; (**38**) making sculpture\Ghana; (**40**) dancers\Senegal; (**43**) a dance done by gold miners\South Africa; (**44**) dancers\Burkina Fasso.

Glossary

Animistic Believing that all things, living and nonliving, have souls.

Circumcision The practice of removing a male's foreskin. Circumcision is usually done for cultural or religious reasons.

Colonization The process in which a country takes over another land and claims it as part of their territory.

Conversion The act of changing from one way of practicing religion to another.

Fetishes Objects used in traditional African religious practices that are believed to contain spiritual powers.

Jok The African concept of a divine spirit that inhabits everything.

Kwanzaa A holiday created in 1966 to celebrate the cultural roots of African Americans.

Monotheistic Believing in the existence of one ruling god or spirit.

Nomadic Having no fixed home. Nomads travel from place to place with their herds in search of new grazing lands.

Pantheistic Believing in the existence of many ruling gods or spirits.

Pilgrimage A journey. Members of the Muslim faith make a pilgrimage to Mecca, the Islamic holy city.

Scarification The practice of ritually scarring a person's body with symbols of patterns that are culturally significant.

Totem An object that has powerful spiritual meaning for a tribe or other large group of people.

Index